All Aboard the Marriage Hearse

by

Matt Morillo

FOUNDED 1830

NEW YORK HOLLYWOOD LONDON TORONTO

SAMUELFRENCH.COM

IMPORTANT BILLING AND CREDIT REQUIREMENTS

All producers of *ALL ABOARD THE MARRIAGE HEARSE must* give credit to the Author of the Play in all programs distributed in connection with performances of the Play, and in all instances in which the title of the Play appears for the purposes of advertising, publicizing or otherwise exploiting the Play and/or a production. The name of the Author *must* appear on a separate line on which no other name appears, immediately following the title and *must* appear in size of type not less than fifty percent of the size of the title type.

EXTRA SPECIAL ACKNOWLEDGEMENT

CRYSTAL FIELD
AND
THEATER FOR THE NEW CITY

We must express our gratitude to Crystal Field and all the fine people at the Theater for the New City. After giving us the opportunity to push *Angry Young Women In Low-Rise Jeans With High-Class Issues* to a higher level in 2007, they once again believed in us and gave us the opportunity to launch *All Aboard the Marriage Hearse* in 2008.

We are proud to say that we delivered another audience-pleasing show which achieved stellar reviews, sold-out houses and great media attention.

However, we are even more proud to be embraced by such a wonderful organization.

We cannot thank them enough for their support and for granting us the opportunity to showcase this play.

Organizations like Theater for the New City are very difficult to find these days, organizations that nurture emerging artists and allow them to grow. Through the years, their commitment to new playwrights and new works has helped launch the careers of many great, well-known playwrights, actors and artists of all kinds. Here's to hoping that we will one day be added to that list!

Once again, a great many thanks to Crystal Field and Theater for the New City. Please support them. They are doing some amazing things.

www.theaterforthenewcity.net

SPECIAL THANKS

Richard West, Sara Steigerwald, Mike Farrell, SuperGrip, The Gorney Family, The Hicksville Crew, Adrian Gallard, Mark Marcante, Angelina Soriano, Don Lewis, Maria Micheles, PIP Printing of Hicksville, Dan Kelley, Jerry Jaffe, Jonathan Weber, Candice Burridge, Chris Force, Ellen Steier, Dan Shearer, Keith Ninesling, Jason Cola, Keon Mohajeri, Jon D. Andreadakis, Richard Reta, Rabbi Shmuley Boteach, Joey Reynolds and the Joey Reynolds Show, Myra Chanin, Kevin Mazeski and of course, all of our friends and family for their support!

ALL ABOARD THE MARRIAGE HEARSE had its world premiere from January 3rd through February 9th of 2008 at the Theater for the New City at 155 1st Avenue in New York City.

The original cast and production team were as follows:

SEAN . . . . Nick Coleman
AMY . . . . Jessica Durdock

Produced by . . . . Jessica Durdock and Matt Morillo
Set Design . . . . Mark Marcante
Lighting Design . . . . Amith A. Chandrashaker
Stage Management . . . . Adrian Gallard
Publicity . . . . Jonathan Slaff and Associates

NOTES FOR PRODUCERS

All licensees are welcome to use the *ALL ABOARD THE MARRIAGE HEARSE* artwork in their marketing materials, although it is not required. It is also not required that producers use the artwork in color, as budget restraints may not allow it. Contact Samuel French Inc. for the materials.

If using the artwork, in the program, the following must be credited:

"The All Aboard the Marriage Hearse artwork is the exclusive property of KADM Productions, LLC. The design was originally created by Sara Steigerwald of www.exquisitebeast.com."

Credit for the playwright must be as follows:

Matt Morillo (Writer) Filmmaker/Playwright Matt Morillo has also written the play, Angry Young Women In Low-Rise Jeans With High-Class Issues (www.angryyoungwomen.net) which was a hit in New York and Sydney, Australia. For more information on his films, visit www.kadm.com. To visit his blog, go to www.thecynicaloptimist.net.

NOTE FOR PRODUCERS: *THE ALL ABOARD THE MARRIAGE HEARSE* set is essentially a living room in an apartment on New York City's Upper East Side. If possible, there should be two functioning doors, one downstage right which serves as the door to the apartment and the other should be upstage left which serves as the door to the bedroom. There should also be a doorway which should lead to an offstage kitchen. A couch in the center of the room is essential, as is a coffee table and a stocked liquor cabinet. As the characters make their journey through the story, they make good use of the doors and the liquor in the liquor cabinet, therefore these are the essential items. Producers should feel free to decorate the set to give it a lived-in, realistic feel.

The play functions best when the actors make good use of the items on set. For example, Amy is the messy one and Sean is the neat one. In some tense moments, in order to avoid the subject, Sean can clean up some clutter. Conversely, in tense moments, Amy can make messes by fussing with the couch pillows, kicking her shoes around or leaving empty glasses around.

CAST OF CHARACTERS

SEAN: Late twenties, handsome, with short, dark hair. Despite his slightly smarmy demeanor, he is very appealing in a boy-next-door kind of way. He is kind of a neat freak and has a tendency to clean up after Amy when he gets frustrated.

AMY: Mid-twenties, very pretty with long flowing brown hair and an approachable beauty. She has a cute/sexy way about her despite her slightly neurotic, boundless energy. She is kind of a slob. She leaves her clothes, shoes, jewelry and coats everywhere.

SCENE

One bedroom apartment on Manhattan's Upper East Side.

TIME

Tonight at midnight.

ACT I

(A nicely decorated living room. The room is not very large, but whoever decorated it made the most of what they had. The couch at center stage is large and comfy with a coffee table in front of it. The coffee table has a bunch of magazines on it. The walls are painted a nice earth tone and there is some art on the walls. The art is not too flashy. It just blends with the rest of the room.

Downstage right is the main door to the apartment. It has a light switch on the wall next to it. Upstage right is a small corridor that leads to the off-stage kitchen and upstage left is the door to the bedroom. Downstage left is a small liquor cabinet with bottles of liquor on top. Under the liquor cabinet is a small stereo system.

The room is dark, lit only by the street light that comes in through the window.)

(Off stage we hear a guy and a girl LAUGHING. We hear keys BANGING together.

The door opens. SEAN and AMY dance their way into the room.

SEAN looks ready for the cover of GQ in his snazzy looking suit, and AMY looks radiant in her purple bridesmaid's gown. She's holding a bouquet of flowers.

SEAN spins her out, and pulls her towards him as he leans up against the door, shutting it.

He sings a romantic song to her as he dances with her. He can't sing.)

AMY. Stop singing.

SEAN. Anything you say I'll do.

AMY. Then why won't you stop singing?

SEAN. Baby, I only want to make you happy.

AMY. Then at least sing a different song.

SEAN. Okay, okay.

(She kisses him. That shuts him up.)

SEAN. You look beautiful tonight. You know that, right?

AMY. Aw. Thank you. You're beautiful too.

SEAN. Beautiful? That's not very masculine.

AMY. Neither is your singing.

(She flips the light switch on, illuminating the room.

They start taking off their coats, jackets, shoes and jewelry. They're making quite a mess with their stuff all over the floor. They're getting ready for action.)

AMY. Didn't Suzanne look gorgeous?

SEAN. She looked okay.

AMY. Brides are always so hot aren't they?

SEAN. You looked better than Suzanne. And you looked better than all the other bridesmaids.

AMY. Oh really? Were you checking them out?

SEAN. No. I'm just saying that you outshined them all. And you caught the bouquet.

AMY. And you caught the garter.

SEAN. They staged that.

AMY. Don't say that.

SEAN. They put me right in front and Pete threw it right at me.

AMY. It was fate.

SEAN. Honey, they wanted us to do the thing.

AMY. It was fate that so many people want us to be together. That's fate. That's kismet.

SEAN. Oh I'll kiss you alright.

(He kisses her and tackles her to the floor and they kiss on the floor for a bit. Sean straddles her, but stops kissing her.)

SEAN. Something's missing.

AMY. You're right. Come on.

(She starts to undo his pants, but he stops her.)

SEAN. How about a little Pulse?

AMY. Pulse?

SEAN. Pink Floyd Pulse.

AMY. You mean that stuff that makes me feel like I'm on acid? No thanks.

SEAN. Alright. Alright.

AMY. How about some Prince?

SEAN. Barry White?

AMY. Deal.

(He hoists her up off the ground and smacks her on the ass. She jumps onto the couch.)

AMY. Hurry. Put the music on. I want to scream and I don't want the neighbors to hear us.

(He laughs.)

AMY. What are you laughing at?

SEAN. You. You're funny.

AMY. What? You don't want the music on?

SEAN. I do. I'll take care of it now.

(Instead of going to the stereo, he runs towards the kitchen.)

AMY. Where are you going?

SEAN. I'll be right back. You just sit right there and I'll be right back and we will pick up right where we left off.

(He runs off stage into the kitchen.

We hear **SEAN** *messing around in the kitchen. Plates are BANGING, glasses are CLINKING.)*

AMY. What are you doing?

SEAN (O.S.) A little surprise for the occasion.

AMY. I hate surprises. You know that.

SEAN (O.S.) You'll like this one.

AMY. Hurry up! I'm calming down.

SEAN (O.S.) Don't. I'm going as fast as I can. The kitchen's a mess.

AMY. Was it my turn to clean?

SEAN (O.S.) Who cares? I'll clean it tomorrow.

AMY. You're the best.

SEAN (O.S.) Just sit tight and stay beautiful.

(She smiles. She's in love. She settles into the couch again. She adjusts her dress. She looks down at her dress as if she just noticed something.)

AMY. This is a nice dress but I don't like the color.

SEAN (O.S.) Why not?

AMY. I would've gone with blue dresses. I like blue. Like a baby blue. That would have been prettier.

SEAN (O.S.) Blue brings out your eyes.

(She grabs the bouquet that she had. She looks at it and smells it.)

AMY. I'd want a ring bearer too. My nephew would be perfect. I'd also pick a nicer place, you know, not such a Guido-looking catering hall.

SEAN (O.S.) You said it was one of the most beautiful ceremonies you've ever seen.

AMY. I know but I could've made it better. I'm good at weddings. I helped plan my sister's and my cousin's, and my friends.

SEAN (O.S.) You should get a job as a wedding planner.

AMY. I also helped with my friend Linda's wedding. Did you ever meet her?

SEAN (O.S.) I don't think so.

AMY. I think she moved right before we started seeing each other. I'd plan a wedding like hers if it was up to me.

*(***SEAN*** comes back into the room with two wine glasses and a bottle of wine.)*

SEAN. Now you're calming me down. I'll have shut you up.

(He jumps on the couch and kisses her. She pulls back.)

AMY. What was calming you down?

SEAN. Nothing.

AMY. The wedding talk was calming you down?

SEAN. I was just joking, I didn't even realize...what do you mean?

AMY. I was talking about weddings and you said you were calming down.

SEAN. I was making a joke based on your joke about calming down. It had nothing to do with what you were talking about.

AMY. What was I talking about?

SEAN. Weddings. You don't need to test me. I was listening. Let's have some wine.

AMY. What about the music?

SEAN. I'll put it on in a minute.

(He pours some in each glass. They toast.)

AMY. Did you say you had a surprise for me?

SEAN. What?

AMY. You said you had a surprise. I know it wasn't the wine.

SEAN. You're right. I knew I forgot something. Where's my brain?

AMY. I wonder about that often.

SEAN. Ha, ha.

(He runs out of the opposite end of the room into the bedroom.)

AMY. Are you going to put the music on finally?

SEAN (O.S.) On my way out. But we have to do this first.

AMY. What exactly are we doing?

(He comes back in, going nowhere near the stereo.)

SEAN. Something I wanted to do at the reception, but it wouldn't have been appropriate. I wouldn't want to take attention away from the bride and groom, you know...

(He grabs her hand and leads her off of the couch. He sits her on the arm of the couch. He grabs a pillow cushion off of the couch and places it on the floor in front of her. He kneels on it. He takes her right leg and lifts over her left leg so that she sits cross-legged.)

SEAN. We're going to do this right.

(He reaches into his back pocket.

Amy's eyes open wide.

He's got something in his hand.)

SEAN. Close your eyes.

(She does.)

AMY. Oh my God. Oh my God.

(He opens his hand, he's holding a scrunchy.

He stretches the scrunchy out and glides it up and down her leg.

He lets out a little playful ROAR.

She opens her eyes.)

AMY. Is that my scrunchy?

SEAN. It'll be a fine replacement.

AMY. For what?

SEAN. The garter.

(He puts it around her ankle.)

AMY. What are you doing?

(He starts moving it up her leg as if it were the garter.

He gets to the knee.)

SEAN. Here were are...

(He moves it up a little more.)

SEAN. In the privacy of our own home.

(He moves it up and it disappears under her dress.

She grabs his hand.)

AMY. What the hell are you doing?

SEAN. What's the matter?

AMY. What's the matter?!

SEAN. Oh, the music.

(He gets up and runs over to the stereo. She watches him incredulously.)

SEAN. What did we agree on? Prince?

(He puts a real funky, sexy song on.

He sways to it a little bit as we makes his way back to the couch. She just stares at him in disbelief. He gets back to the couch.

He leans down to mount her, but she gets up at the last minute, causing him to land on the empty couch.)

AMY. Are you kidding?

SEAN. What? Oh. We agreed on Barry White, didn't we?

(He runs back to the stereo, shuts off the music and searches for another CD.)

AMY. Are you deliberately messing with me?

SEAN. No. I just made a mistake.

AMY. Yes. You did.

SEAN. Relax. I'm switching the CD.

AMY. I'm not talking about the music.

SEAN. Well you've lost me.

AMY. I'm talking about what was just about to happen.

SEAN. About to happen?

AMY. I thought you were going to propose.

SEAN. Propose what?

AMY. What do you think?

SEAN. Are you kidding?

AMY. Well you kind of set the scene for it.

SEAN. No I didn't. I was just trying to make this nice and romantic.

AMY. I see that and I thought you were getting romantic because you were about to...you know.

SEAN. Alright, time out. How many years have we been dating?

AMY. That has nothing to do with this.

SEAN. How many years have we been living together?

AMY. I'm not playing this game.

SEAN. How many times have you been made aware of how I feel about this subject?

AMY. Well perhaps in our nearly three wonderful years together, you changed your mind.

SEAN. I didn't.

AMY. Then you just messed with me.

SEAN. I was trying to have fun. Recreate the little event from earlier and then take it to its natural conclusion.

AMY. What would that be? Removing my panties from under my dress?

SEAN. I guess that eventually would have to happen.

AMY. What is wrong with you?

SEAN. Nothing. A minute ago we were having a great time and then –

AMY. You decided to mess with me.

SEAN. Alright, alright. Let's stop. I'm sorry. We were having a really nice evening and I was just trying to keep it going. I didn't mean to mess with you. I swear.

AMY. Okay. I'm sorry too. I got a little caught up in all the wedding stuff and my head went a little crazy.

SEAN. I understand. Weddings are like porn for women. It scrambles your guys' brains a bit.

(He sits next to her on the couch and kisses her.)

AMY. Wait. Stop.

(She pushes him away.)

AMY. Weddings are like porn for women? What kind of comment was that?

SEAN. It was a joke.

AMY. Why haven't you changed your mind about this?

SEAN. Come on. Let's not to this now.

AMY. Answer the question.

SEAN. If I answer, can we move past this?

AMY. Yes we can.

SEAN. Fine. There are some things about me that are never going to change. That's one of them.

AMY. That's your answer?

SEAN. Yes.

AMY. Wrong answer.

SEAN. Wrong answer?

AMY. Wrong answer.

SEAN. *(to himself)* Why didn't I just put the damn music on?

AMY. Your mistake.

SEAN. Yeah. I feel like I'm back in high school.

AMY. So do I. I'm dealing with a boy who is saying anything to shut me up and get laid.

SEAN. What is with you?

AMY. I don't like your answer so I'm not in the mood anymore.

SEAN. Do you care to fill me in on what the right answer would've been?

AMY. No. But I will ask a follow up question. Why is that one thing about you that will never change?

SEAN. I'm not doing this.

(He gets off the couch and heads to the liquor cabinet.)

AMY. You started this.

SEAN. How did I start this?

(He pours himself a big glass of scotch.)

AMY. You got on your knees in front of a bridesmaid who just got home from her friend's wedding in which she caught the bouquet and you caught the garter and then you hid your hands behind your back saying you have a surprise for her. How could you not expect me to see that as a proposal?

SEAN. Oh come on. In this living room, on that couch, with no champagne and just some cheap white wine? That would've been the lamest proposal ever. How the hell could you mistake THAT for a proposal?

AMY. I thought maybe it was the best I was going to get from you.

SEAN. Well the point is moot anyway because you should've known better because you are well aware of how I feel about this.

AMY. And you're well aware of how I feel so you should've known better.

SEAN. We're both well aware of how each other feels and that's why this conversation should end now.

AMY. I want to know why you refuse to change your mind about this.

SEAN. I could ask you the same question.

AMY. I won't answer unless you answer first.

SEAN. Let's not go there. You're just going to get upset.

AMY. I'm already upset.

SEAN. Okay. But this is the last time that we will ever discuss this. Agreed?

AMY. Agreed.

SEAN. I'm serious, Amy.

AMY. So am I.

SEAN. Okay. Here we go.

(He downs the entire glass of scotch.)

AMY. Ew.

SEAN. I do not believe in marriage. I never have. I never will. It's an outdated, archaic institution that was invented in a time when people married at fifteen and only lived to be thirty. Furthermore, it is a religious institution and neither one of us is religious. So I'm not hypocrite enough to do something like that. It is also completely unnecessary. We already live together, we already have a joint bank account, we sleep together and we sleep only with each other, if we want we can have papers drawn up by a lawyer leaving each other everything. I have health insurance from my job and you have it from your job so we don't have to worry about all the bullshit "benefits" that they try to wave in people's faces to entice them to get married. You know, I am not the first person to come up with this idea. I am far from the first. But for some asinine reason, it just hasn't caught on yet. Okay?

AMY. Okay.

SEAN. So we're cool?

AMY. We're real cool. And we'll be even cooler if we get married.

SEAN. No. We'll be totally uncool, like a fat kid in high school.

AMY. I'm not joking anymore, Sean. I want this.

SEAN. Why?

AMY. Why not?

SEAN. It's pointless. We're already committed to each other.

AMY. I want to hear you say it in front of a priest.

SEAN. Oh come on. I don't believe in the Catholic church and you're a Jew.

AMY. A justice of the peace then.

SEAN. You're just grasping at straws now.

AMY. We can have an interfaith wedding with a rabbi and a priest.

SEAN. I can't believe I'm having this conversation. We're not having any wedding and...what is with all this priest and rabbi shit? You don't even believe in God.

AMY. I never said that.

SEAN. When was the last time you went to temple for something other than a wedding or a funeral or a Shiva or whatever you people call it?

AMY. I go with my mom sometimes.

SEAN. Because she guilts you into it.

AMY. I'm not going to let you turn this into one of your religious rants.

SEAN. You brought it up.

AMY. The point is that I want to get married and I want a nice wedding and I want to marry you and you are being so unfair to me about this.

SEAN. Me? You knew how I felt about this before we even started dating. When I met you, you told me that you read my column from time to time and you even said you read my Marriage Hearse article. So I know you knew how I felt.

AMY. Yes I did but –

SEAN. But you thought that you could change that?

AMY. I never looked that far ahead.

SEAN. But now you want to look that far ahead?

AMY. No. I'm living in the now. And right now we live together, we have fun, we love each other, and we have all those things you mentioned. The only thing we don't have is –

SEAN. A sanction from the government or some cult. And I'm not interested in that.

(**SEAN** *pours himself another glass of scotch.*)

AMY. What are you worried about? Will your readers think you're a sell out?

SEAN. My readers?

AMY. I know you try to be "Mr. Anti-Establishment Super Cynic." How would your loyal readers feel if their favorite smarmy columnist walked down the aisle and said "I do."

SEAN. This has nothing to do with that and you know what, while we're at it, why don't you pull out my Marriage Hearse column.

AMY. I've read it so many times it makes me sick.

SEAN. Then why are we having this conversation?

AMY. Because we're in a relationship, and when you are in a relationship you discuss and compromise your disagreements.

SEAN. Let's just stop this right now. You're all emotional because we just got back from the wedding and everything. So let's calm down and continue this some other time.

AMY. We already agreed that this is the last time we'll ever have this conversation. So we're going to finish this. And you're going to change your mind.

SEAN. Why can't YOU change your mind?

AMY. Because I want the same thing as you. I want to spend the rest of my life with you.

SEAN. But you have a different way you want to do it.

AMY. Yes and it's very selfish of you to deny me that just because your parents had a miserable marriage.

SEAN. Oh stop. Just stop. Only an idiot would base their opinion of something like this on just one example.

AMY. You said it not me.

SEAN. Do you think that this is about my parents?

AMY. I know it is. Every time you get drunk I have to hear you, "I'm not like my father. I'm not like my father."

SEAN. That's right. I'm not.

AMY. I know you're not. So cut the bullshit and let's get married.

SEAN. Why do you want to risk all this?

AMY. What's the risk? I always said, since I was a little girl that I would never get married unless I absolutely knew that I was with the right guy.

SEAN. Don't you think everyone "knows?" Don't you think that my mother "knew" my father was the right guy? Don't you think that out of the sixty percent of couples that get divorced, don't you think they all "knew" they were with the right person?

AMY. Why are you mentioning your mother?

SEAN. She's a good example.

AMY. Oh, but you don't base your opinion on marriage on your parents?

SEAN. No I don't. I've seen successful marriages. My

grandparents were in love with each other until the day they died. They were like teenagers when they were in their seventies.

AMY. Why can't you base your opinion of this on them?

SEAN. Are you listening to me? I don't base my opinion on any one couple. And you know what, I can give you reasons for the next twelve days why I don't believe in marriage and I've said enough. So now I want you to give me one legitimate reason why we should get married?

AMY. What about –

SEAN. Something other than a romantic cliche.

AMY. What about –

SEAN. Just one reason.

AMY. I'm giving it to you. Shut up. What about children?

SEAN. What about them?

AMY. You don't think it's better for them to be raised by a married couple and have that security?

SEAN. What security?

AMY. The security that one of their parents won't just walk away at anytime and the knowledge that their parents have to stick things out.

SEAN. Actually I think it's worse for kids when they see their parents stay together just for them. That teaches them bad lessons. It teaches them that people should stay together no matter what. That's what fucked up our generation and our parents, and our grandparents.

AMY. Oh God. Can we assume for a moment that WE will have a happy marriage and can you at least agree that it's good for kids if they're brought up in a happy marriage?

SEAN. It's no different than if they were raised in a happy relationship and as long as we're in a happy relationship, you're not going anywhere and neither am I.

AMY. But if we ever become unhappy you or I could just walk away at any time if we're not married.

SEAN. And that's better for the kids too. They get to learn that people fall in love and out of love. It's a good lesson to learn young.

AMY. It did wonders for you.

SEAN. Alright. Are you going to give me a good reason for us to get married or is it bedtime?

AMY. I gave you one.

SEAN. I refuted it.

AMY. I just want it.

SEAN. You just want it?

AMY. That's right.

SEAN. So I have to go on trial to justify my point of view but you can say "I just want it?"

AMY. It's the natural order of things. When you're with someone for a long time and you love each other and you're committed to each other, it's the next step. It's just like when you start a company. You incorporate.

SEAN. So you're comparing love to forming a corporation?

AMY. That's what it's like.

SEAN. And you don't see the absurdity in that? Something as unexplainable and mysterious as love, you're willing to break it down to a written contract? Like we're AOL/Time Warner or something.

AMY. Oh please. Like you're some kind of pure romantic.

SEAN. I am. I believe what Oscar Wilde said. He said, "the very essence of love is uncertainty, and marriage takes all the uncertainty out of it."

AMY. He was gay.

SEAN. What does that have to do with anything?

AMY. He had no frame of reference. He was never married.

SEAN. You were never married. What makes you think it's so great?

AMY. What we have is great and I'd like to take it to the next level.

SEAN. Why do you think that's the only way to do it?

AMY. I don't know. I just do.

SEAN. Well I'm going to tell you why. Ever since you were a little girl, you have been told that one day you would have this grand event where you get to look all beautiful and your daddy walks you down the aisle and you get to be princess for a day. For your entire life, the idea of getting married has been packaged and sold to you like Coca-Cola.

AMY. Yeah. So?

SEAN. That doesn't bother you?

AMY. It's a tradition. There's nothing wrong with traditions.

SEAN. Sometimes there's a lot wrong with traditions. Society evolves and outgrows them. It's time to outgrow this one.

AMY. I think it's a nice one. We can have a big party and –

SEAN. We can do that now.

AMY. We'll have an anniversary.

SEAN. We have one

AMY. We'll have a real one.

SEAN. What do we have now? A fake one?

AMY. You know what I mean.

SEAN. Let me ask you this. Have you ever considered not getting married?

AMY. I'm not childish enough to lose faith in something so beautiful just because a lot of people screw it up.

SEAN. And there's a reason they all screw it up and I'm going to tell you what it is.

AMY. Somehow I knew you would.

SEAN. Unmarried people, who are happy like you and me, we make a conscious choice every morning. Every day, we choose to stay with each other because we love each other. We don't do it because of a promise we made in front of a man in a big white robe. The married people go on auto pilot. Little by little, they stop working at their relationship, no matter how much they swore they wouldn't. They stop working because the marriage contract is there. The guarantee is there.

AMY. I won't stop working at it. I promise.

SEAN. You can't make that promise and neither can I.

AMY. Why can't we just get married, and you can continue to pretend that we're not?

SEAN. Are you listening to yourself?

AMY. Unfortunately I've been listening to you and it's giving me a headache.

SEAN. Then let's stop this and go to bed.

(He starts for the bedroom.)

AMY. Don't you dare. I'm not done.

(He stops. She gets up and walks right into his space.)

AMY. In the time we've been together, have I done everything in my power to make you happy?

SEAN. Yes.

AMY. And I know that you have done everything you could to make me happy. Why are you willing to stop here?

SEAN. I'm not, I'm –

AMY. Shut up. I didn't want to move in here into your grandmother's apartment but I did. I wanted you to move in with me in Astoria. But you had to be in Manhattan. I didn't want to lie to your crazy mother about us living together. But I did it. When Patrick's wife caught him drinking again and threw him out, I didn't want him to stay here for three months. But I kept my mouth shut because I knew how close of a friend he was to you.

SEAN. And I would've done any of those things for you.

AMY. My point is that when you are in a relationship, you compromise. You do whatever you have to do to make your partner happy. I don't think I'm asking for a lot. All I want is for you to make a promise, a promise that you have already made to me. I just want you to do it in front of some other people.

SEAN. Why isn't the promise I made to you alone good enough?

AMY. I deserve more. I'm a good person and I've busted my ass to support you and help you have your dreams come true. Who –

(He starts towards the bedroom.)

AMY. Where are you going?

SEAN. I'd like to change out of this suit.

AMY. I am talking.

(He disappears into the bedroom.)

SEAN. I can hear you from in here.

AMY. Get out here right now!

(He relents and comes out of the bedroom, looking defeated.)

SEAN. Do you want me to stand in the corner?

AMY. Sit down.

(He sits on the couch.)

AMY. So, like I was saying, who supported you when the Voice fired you? I did. Who stroked your pathetic little crushed ego? I did. Who helped you get the job at the New Yorker? I did. When you broke your hand, who typed all of your columns for you? I did. And now you've got everything you want. Everything you want. You've got a job you love, a good salary, a popular column and a book about to be published. I have my teaching job, a great family and you. I have everything I want except one thing. And the one person I love more than anyone on the planet is the one person who can give it to me. But he won't.

SEAN. I don't have everything I want. I want to live a life that's just a little bit different than everyone elses. I want to be with someone – no, I want to be with you. I want to wake up one morning about forty or fifty years from now and look at you and say, "Wow, we made it. We did it. We stuck together. And we did it because we wanted to, not because we said we would."

AMY. We can do that. We can also do it in front of the proper authorities.

SEAN. Oh Christ, don't you think I understand what you're going through?

AMY. I don't think you possibly can. I don't think you possibly can understand what it feels like to be among the last of the teachers at that school who isn't married. You can't understand what it's like when kids ask, "why are you Miss and not Mrs.?" Or what it's like to hear the other teachers plan weddings and constantly ask, "when are you guys gonna do it?" Or what's it's like at parent-teacher conferences to sit with these people and know that they don't really respect me because I'm not married yet. And I don't even want to get into what it will be like if we ever have a baby and I'm still MISS Cohen. That will be fun explaining that to a class of eight-year olds. I'm in an environment where they still take these values seriously and whether you like it or not, this could all affect my career.

SEAN. First of all, you're tenured, so you'd have to molest one of these kids for them to ever fire you and you know that. Second, let's not act like you teach in the Bible belt. You teach in Queens and that's not that conservative. And lastly, I understand all that stuff. The pressure's not as intense for guys, but we are given the same shit. If you choose to not get married, all you hear are people saying, "oh well you haven't grown up yet. You haven't settled down." As if deciding to get married has something to do with maturity. But at least I've questioned it. I'm choosing to go against it.

AMY. At my expense.

SEAN. To your benefit. You and I are going to be so much happier and so much more fulfilled in our relationship than all of our married friends if we just stay on the path we're on.

AMY. I won't be happy on the path we're on.

SEAN. You won't even open your mind to it.

AMY. And you won't open your mind to what I want.

SEAN. How can you say that? You can't grow up in our society without the assumption that you one day will get married. I once considered it and decided that it's not a good idea. Did you ever open the same inquiry?

AMY. With every single boyfriend I've ever had.

SEAN. That's not what I asked you. I know you've considered whether you should marry this person or that person, but have you just ever considered the idea of not getting married?

AMY. No.

SEAN. I rest my case.

AMY. Have you ever cheated on me?

SEAN. What? Where did that come from?

AMY. Answer the question.

SEAN. I have never cheated on you.

AMY. Will you ever?

SEAN. No.

AMY. Do you promise?

SEAN. Yes.

AMY. Do you swear?

SEAN. Yes.

AMY. I trust you. I believe you.

SEAN. Thank you.

AMY. Do you think I'd ever cheat on you?

SEAN. I wouldn't be with you if I did.

AMY. It looks like all our questions are answered. So if you would just drop the semantics and agree to get married, we can go to bed and put this miserable evening behind us.

SEAN. So you want me to agree to get married, even though I don't believe in it? Even though it would be meaningless to me?

AMY. It would mean something to me.

SEAN. What exactly would it mean?

AMY. Like I said earlier. If we have kids, I would know that you couldn't just up and leave me if times get tough.

SEAN. And like I said earlier, if we were married, I could always leave you then too, couldn't I?

AMY. You couldn't do it as easily.

SEAN. So you see marriage as a trap?

AMY. YOU see it as a trap. I see it as the ultimate expression of love.

SEAN. I see it as the ultimate expression of fear.

AMY. Fear?

SEAN. Yes, fear. "I am so afraid that you will leave me one day that I'm going to lock you down to a contract to make sure that you never do, but if you do, I will make it so hard for you that it will not be worth your time. Then we can just live in quiet desperation and wait to die." That is what marriage is. And somewhere deep down, you know it and that's why you're so upset.

AMY. I'm upset because you're an ass hole.

(She darts to the liquor cabinet and pours herself a glass of scotch.)

SEAN. Then why do you want to marry me so bad?

AMY. I'm starting to wonder that myself. Maybe we should just call it quits.

SEAN. Call it quits?

AMY. That's right. We obviously want different things out of life.

SEAN. This has gotten out of hand. We don't want different things. We are both very tired, very emotional and we've both had plenty to drink tonight. I suggest we go to bed and I'm sure that in the morning we'll forget all about this conversation.

AMY. I'm sure we will. And you'll weasel your way out of this and you'll get your way because we already agreed to never bring it up again.

SEAN. I'm not weasling my way out of anything. I'm not breaking any agreements that we made. I am exactly the same guy I was when you met me.

AMY. Maybe that's the problem. People should change. They should evolve.

SEAN. Then how can they ever commit their lives to each other?

AMY. They change together. They evolve togehter. They –

SEAN. Oh God. Come on.

AMY. Goddammit, Sean. I know you don't want this and I know you said it from the beginning. But you know that I'm a girl and that this would come up. How did you not think of that?

SEAN. I just...I just...Alright, I'll tell you what. I'll make you a deal. Let's go rent a car right now, drive to Vegas and get married.

AMY. What?

SEAN. That's a compromise. Relationships are about compromise, right?

AMY. How much have you had to drink?

SEAN. I'm serious about this. Let's do it.

AMY. So you won't make this promise in front of a priest or a rabbi but you'll do it in front of Elvis?

SEAN. Not every chapel has an Elvis in it.

AMY. Yes, honey. Let's do it. Great idea. On the way to our wedding we can pass casinos and strip clubs. I can't wait.

SEAN. If you want me to do this, that's the way I want to do it. It's different. Actually, it's kind of romantic. A cross country drive and then we come back and tell everyone that we're married.

AMY. That's ridiculous.

SEAN. How is it anymore ridiculous than what you want to do?

AMY. Because normal people want what I want.

SEAN. We're not normal people.

AMY. No. You're not.

SEAN. I think that's a compliment.

AMY. I'm sure you do.

SEAN. This is your last chance. Do you want to do the Vegas thing or not?

AMY. I'd rather spend an afternoon with your mother.

SEAN. Alright. This is getting ugly.

AMY. Your mother's ugly.

SEAN. And I think it's time for bed.

(He takes his empty glass off the table and heads into the kitchen.

AMY *sips from her scotch, waiting for him to return.*

SEAN *emerges from the kitchen. He heads straight for the bedroom, trying not to look at her.)*

AMY. Are you serious about the Vegas offer?

SEAN. Sure.

AMY. Or are you saying it because you know I'll never agree to it?

SEAN. If you want to do this, this is how I want to do it.

AMY. Okay.

(She downs her scotch.)

SEAN. Okay what?

AMY. Let's go.

SEAN. Let's go where?

AMY. Put your coat on. First I want you to call your mother and tell her what we're doing.

SEAN. What exactly are we doing?

AMY. We're going to rent a car, drive to Vegas and get married.

SEAN. You're joking.

AMY. It's your idea. If that's the only way I can get you to make this commitment, so be it. Come on.

(She puts her coat on.)

AMY. Make the call. Come on. Let's go.

(**SEAN** *picks up the phone. He dials.*

AMY *starts picking her shoes and jewelry up off the floor and puts it all back on.*)

SEAN. Hello, ma. It's me. I know it's late but – I know. But I'm calling for something important. No, it can't wait. Amy and me are driving to Vegas tonight. We're geting married. No, I'm not kidding. I just want you to know. Alright, alright. I'm sorry. I'm sorry. Call me later.

AMY. What did she say?

SEAN. Nothing.

AMY. Why were you apologizing to her?

SEAN. She was mad that I called during Saturday Night Live.

AMY. Let's go.

(**SEAN** *looks like he's walking in water as he slowly walks towards the bedroom.*)

AMY. Why are you moving so slow?

SEAN. Don't you think we should change out of these clothes first?

AMY. Why bother trying to look normal? Let's go.

SEAN. Let's at least pack a bag.

AMY. And give you a chance to change your mind? No thanks. We'll pick up essentials on the way. Let's go.

SEAN. Do you really want this?

AMY. Sure. I'm willing to give up everything I ever dreamed about just so you don't have to put on a tux and take pictures.

SEAN. I think we're both a little emotional right now and –

AMY. If you say that one more time I'm going to slap you.

SEAN. How are we going to rent a car? We've both been drinking.

AMY. You're unbelievable.

SEAN. I don't think getting arrested would be a good idea for either of us.

AMY. This whole thing was bullshit.

SEAN. I don't think we should be making any impulsive decisions.

AMY. After all this time together, this is hardly impulsive.

SEAN. Just think about it.

AMY. I knew you were lying.

(She starts taking off her coat and jewelry again, tossing them on the floor in anger.)

SEAN. I wasn't lying.

AMY. You offered that because you thought I wouldn't agree to it.

SEAN. Oh please. You would've changed your mind by the time we hit Jersey.

AMY. Do you want to test me?

SEAN. I want to go to bed.

AMY. I'm not going to sleep tonight. Not a bit.

(She angrily tosses her shoes towards the door, hitting the wall.

SEAN *runs over and starts picking up after her in his frustration.)*

SEAN. You're going to lose sleep because I won't agree to engage in a dumb tradition that has a sixty percent fail rate?

AMY. We'll fall into the forty.

SEAN. Oh really? And out of the forty, how many of them do you think are happy?

AMY. We will be.

SEAN. We're happy now and we shouldn't jeopardize it. Somewhere deep down you know that marriage ruins almost every good relationship but for some reason you're willing to take that chance.

AMY. Because I love you.

SEAN. And have you ever considered for one minute that the reason I won't do this is because I love you? And because I love you so much, I'm not willing to risk everything we've built just so we can throw a party and refer to each other as husband and wife.

AMY. Nothing has to change. It's just a change of labels.

SEAN. If it's just a change of labels why should we bother?

AMY. I want the labels to change.

SEAN. But you still can't give me a good reason why.

AMY. Neither can you.

SEAN. Are you insane? I've given you –

AMY. You've given me a million reasons about how it's stupid and how we're basically already married. So if we're basically already married, why can't you just do this for me?

SEAN. Because I can't.

AMY. It's easy. We stand in front of a group of people and some kind of authority, and we tell each other that we love each other and that we promise to keep loving each other and that we promise to spend the rest of our lives together.

SEAN. I can't do that. And neither can you.

AMY. What are you saying now?

SEAN. I can't promise that I'm going to spend the rest of my life with you. *(She looks at him in disbelief.)* And you can't promise me that either.

AMY. Yes I can. And so can you. You already have.

SEAN. No I didn't. I've said that I WANT to spend the rest of my life with you. It's different.

AMY. Well, I've made that promise to you.

SEAN. But you can't mean it. Because you don't know. And neither do I. And that's why I can't do this.

AMY. I meant it. I mean it now. And I can't believe you're saying this to me.

SEAN. Look, I love you and I'm crazy about you and I can't imagine my life without you. But one day, I can fall out of love with you and you can fall out of love with me. It happens everyday around the world to people all the time. This is what I've been trying to tell you.

AMY. So I've been living a lie with you all this time?

SEAN. No. I just told you that I'm crazy about you. But I will never lie to you. And I won't lock you down into a contract. What if you fall out of love with me one day? Should I be able to just hold you here? And what if I fall out of love with you one day? Would you want to keep me around? I mean, sure we can promise to stay with each other forever and I guess we can follow through on that, but we can't promise to be in love with each other forever. No one can.

AMY. That's the most ridiculous thing I've ever heard.

SEAN. That's because no one ever has the balls to speak the truth. We all just speak in fairy tales.

AMY. I believe in fairy tales.

SEAN. I know you do. It's one of the things I love about you. But I can't promise you this anymore than I can promise that I'll live to be a hundred.

AMY. And you're not even willing to try?

SEAN. Isn't that what we're doing here? Aren't we in a relationship and we're trying to stay with each other forever?

AMY. I don't even know right now.

SEAN. You're just upset. You don't think I know how you feel? They lied to me too. They lie to all of us all the time. They lie to us about love, sex, God, people, everything! For Christ's sake, they lie to us right away and tell us about Santa Claus. At least they have the decency to tell us that Santa is a myth when we're old enough. How old do we have to be for them to tell us marriage is a myth?

AMY. Marriage is a myth?

SEAN. It's Santa Claus for adults.

AMY. Sounds like the name of one of your columns.

SEAN. Honey, let's go to bed. I have a massive headache.

AMY. So do I.

SEAN. So let's go to bed. We've both had a lot to drink.

(She walks away from him and sits on the couch.)

AMY. Do you feel better now? Do you feel smarter now? I do want to look beautiful and be the princess for a day. I do want to book a church or a temple and a catering hall. I do want to pick out flowers. I do want to see you in a tux. I do want my dad to walk me down the aisle and ask me seven times whether I'm sure I want to do this. I do want to see my mother crying in the front row. I do want to see your crazy mother rolling her eyes because she thinks you could've done better. I do want to hear my sister give a speech and I do want to hear Patrick try to make a speech through his drunken stupor. I do want everyone to throw rice at us and I do want them to play that stupid song when we cut the cake and I do want to shove it in your face and I do want to take pictures and I do want you to change your mind about this. And you should give it to me especially since it means nothing to you.

(He sits next to her and puts his arm around her, trying to console her.)

SEAN. I'm sorry.

AMY. You're not sorry at all. You're going to get your way again.

SEAN. This is not about me getting my way.

AMY. I think it is.

SEAN. Look, we're both tired and drunk –

AMY. Don't say that again!

SEAN. What?

AMY. That we're tired and drunk.

SEAN. We are.

(She slaps him hard across the face.

He turns away from her and gets up off the couch.

She can't look at him.

He leaves the room and heads into the kitchen.

SEAN *returns with a glass of water. He approaches the*

couch and offers it to her.)

AMY. I don't want it.

SEAN. Take a sip.

AMY. Leave me alone.

(He takes a seat next to her.)

(Beat.)

AMY. Look at me. Were you serious about the Vegas thing?

SEAN. No.

AMY. I knew it.

(She gets up off the couch and heads for the bedroom.

He starts to follow her out.

She turns around and sees him approaching.)

AMY. Where do you think you're going?

SEAN. To bed.

AMY. I don't want you in bed with me tonight. You take the couch.

SEAN. Come on, honey.

AMY. Go to hell.

SEAN. Look, I want to spend the rest of my life with you. And I'm going to give you everything I have and I will never be with anyone else while I'm with you. That's the best deal I can offer you. And that's the best deal you can offer me.

AMY. I'm willing to offer you more.

(She goes into the bedroom and SLAMS the door.)

SEAN. Can I get my leg pillow?

*(The bedroom door opens. **AMY** comes out with his leg pillow and slams it to the ground.*

She heads back into the bedroom and SLAMS the door again.

***SEAN** begins setting the couch up for sleeping purposes.*

The phone RINGS. It RINGS again.

SEAN *ignores it.*

It RINGS again.

Finally, he answers.)

SEAN. Hello. No, ma. We weren't serious. No I don't think it was funny. We were just having a drunken conversation and it got out of hand. No, it wasn't her idea either. She wasn't trying to make a fool of you.

(**AMY** *marches out of the bedroom. She grabs the phone away from him.)*

AMY. Get over yourself, Maureen. Not everything is about you. Oh yeah? Is that right? Well you know what? You have raised yourself one screwed up son. I hope you're proud of yourself, you crazy old broad.

(She hangs up.)

SEAN. Nice.

AMY. After all this, I really don't need to hear your mother complaining about me.

SEAN. She wasn't complaining about you.

AMY. You were making excuses for what we did.

SEAN. I had to. Can you imagine getting the phone call she got?

(The phone starts RINGING again.)

AMY. If my son called me and told me he was getting married, I wouldn't tell him to wait until Letterman was over.

SEAN. It was Saturday Night Live.

AMY. Shut up.

SEAN. And did you have to call her a crazy old broad?

AMY. Yes I did.

SEAN. Who even says broad anymore?

(She runs over to the base of the phone and tries to tear it out of the wall.

But it won't come out.

It just keeps RINGING.

Finally, she tears the chords out of the back. That stops the ringing.

She heads back into the bedroom with the phone.)

SEAN. Where are you going with the phone?

AMY. This phone is mine.

SEAN. What? Now I can't use your stuff?

(She SLAMS the door shut again.

The stage goes dark.)

END OF ACT I

ACT II

(The lights come up. Sun shines through the window.

SEAN, *now dressed in boxers and an undershirt, sleeps on the couch. An empty bottle of whiskey is on the floor near him.*

The apartment door is open. The apartment looks bare. Paintings are missing, the coffee table that was in front of the couch is missing.

In place of the coffee table is a bottle of aspirin and a glass of water.

AMY, *dressed in jeans and a tee shirt, enters through the apartment door. She walks past the couch, ignoring* **SEAN**. *She goes right into the bedroom.*

A loud THUD is heard off stage. **SEAN** *wakes up. He looks around.*

He notices the door is open. He gives a weird look as he notices the coffee table is gone.)

SEAN. Amy.

(No answer.)

SEAN. Are you okay?

(She comes out of the bedroom with a box in hand.)

AMY. I'm fine.

SEAN. What is that?

AMY. My books.

SEAN. What are you doing with them?

AMY. I'm bringing them to my mother's.

SEAN. Why?

AMY. I'm moving out. By the way, you can keep the bed and that ugly couch. I never liked them.

SEAN. You're moving out?

AMY. I think it's for the best.

SEAN. And you're going to move out today?

AMY. I'm pretty much done. My mother already took one

carload of stuff and she's coming back to get me and the rest of the stuff, which is piled up in the lobby right now. Except of course for this box.

SEAN. You're kidding.

AMY. Go look in the bedroom. Go ahead.

SEAN. Okay.

(He gets up from the couch and takes a step, but he stumbles a little and grabs his temples.)

SEAN. Whoa.

AMY. Great idea polishing off that bottle of whiskey. I left some aspirin and water on the floor for you.

SEAN. I'm okay.

AMY. Great.

(He goes into the bedroom.)

SEAN (O.S.) You moved everything out!

AMY. I told you.

(He charges back in to the room.)

SEAN. You did all this while I was sleeping?

AMY. You snored through the whole thing.

SEAN. You didn't think to wake me and discuss this?

AMY. We discussed everything last night.

SEAN. This is a little crazy.

AMY. Hardly. It's the right thing to do. I realized that you're right.

SEAN. Right about what?

AMY. Everything we discussed.

SEAN. Okay. So why are you leaving?

AMY. I stayed up all night and thought about everything we talked about, and I actually re-read some of your columns too and I realized that you're right and I need to start over.

SEAN. It doesn't look like you did a lot of thinking or reading. It looks like you did a lot of packing.

AMY. Women can multi-task. Now if you'll excuse me...

SEAN. You thought about this all night and your answer is walking out?

AMY. You have a better one?

SEAN. Yes. Stay.

AMY. How is that better?

SEAN. We can talk.

AMY. No.

SEAN. Why no?

AMY. Because you're smarter than me and I'm not interested in being outsmarted again.

SEAN. I'm not smarter than you and I won't try to outsmart you.

AMY. You're doing it now.

SEAN. No I'm not.

AMY. I am leaving now. Take care.

(She leaves, shutting the door behind her.)

SEAN. Amy!

(No answer)

SEAN. Amy!

(No answer.

The apartment key comes sliding out from under the apartment door.

SEAN *is stunned. He looks around the apartment.*

He walks over to the little table that used to hold the phone.

The phone is gone.)

SEAN. Amy, wait!

(He grabs his pants off of the floor and hurriedly puts them on.

He runs to the door.

He opens it.)

SEAN. Amy!

(She's gone.

He shuts the door and runs back towards the couch.

He grabs his suit jacket off the floor. He reaches into the pocket and pulls his cell phone out. He dials.

An annoying cell phone song PLAYS. She left her phone here.

SEAN *looks around.*

It's coming from the liquor cabinet.

He throws his phone down in frustration, stopping the ring. He grabs her phone from the liquor cabinet.)

SEAN. Goddamnit.

(He sits on the couch, defeated.

A KNOCK at the door.

SEAN *springs to life and goes over and opens the door.*

It's **AMY** *of course.*

She comes in.)

AMY. I forgot my cell.

(She looks around a bit for it. She can't find it.

She sees it in Sean's hand.)

AMY. I have to meet my mother downstairs. Please give it to me.

SEAN. When is she coming?

AMY. In about ten minutes or so.

SEAN. Then we have some time to talk.

AMY. There's nothing to talk about. Give me my phone.

SEAN. Not until you explain to me why you are doing this.

AMY. You know why.

SEAN. Because of last night?

AMY. Last night you gave me the answer I needed to hear and I'm glad.

SEAN. You're glad?

AMY. All my life, I believed in the fairy tale of "the one." Every guy I've ever dated I wondered, "is it him? is it him?" And I made myself sick over it and I probably drove everyone one of those guys crazy.

SEAN. You never drove me crazy.

AMY. Let me finish. But it wasn't until last night that I realized, how cynical that idea is. How cynical is it to suggest that in a world of six billion people, there is only one person that can make you happy? How silly is that? And how crazy do we all make ourselves wondering about that? How much extra unnecessary pressure does that put on relationships? Then we feel this inclination to commit our entire lives to this person because we foolishly believe that they are the only one that could ever make us happy. Well, I'm no longer going to be a slave to that train of thought. So with the next guy I date, I won't put that pressure on him or myself. I'll just live day by day and whatever happens, happens. Perhaps there is no such thing as "the one." Just the one for right now.

SEAN. Alright. Stop this. We both know that we're each the one for right now.

AMY. No. We were each the one for the past two years and nine months, until last night. But stop interrupting me because I'm trying to thank you. Thanks to you, this break up is going to be much easier to take for me. I won't get absorbed in the drama of it all. I'll do my crying, and move on to the next guy. Now please give me my phone.

SEAN. No.

(She reaches for it but he holds it up over his head so she can't reach it.)

AMY. You're being silly.

SEAN. I am? You're making up this whole philosophy and you're blaming it on me. All I said was that I didn't believe in marriage. I don't know where you got all this other stuff from.

(He runs away from the door and she chases him until they wind up on opposite sides of the couch.)

AMY. I told you. I re-read a bunch of our columns and I thought you made a lot of good points in them.

SEAN. I never said any of that stuff in my columns.

AMY. No, but you made a lot of points about marriage and relationships and they made me think and I came up with my own theories.

(She runs after him. He runs around the couch. She chases him around the couch a couple of times as they have this argument.)

SEAN. Honey, you're talking crazy.

AMY. For the past few years, I thought you were just a cynic who just needed to find that someone special who could get through to you and steal your heart and make you love life. Now that was crazy.

SEAN. But you did that. You stole my heart and you did make me love life.

AMY. Great. So you're in great shape for the next girl you meet. You're welcome. Phone please.

SEAN. Amy, it's not a good idea to make big decisions when you're upset.

(Finally, they stop on opposite ends of the couch.)

AMY. I'm not upset.

SEAN. Of course you are. You're moving out.

AMY. Do I look upset?

SEAN. Yes.

AMY. This was a well thought out decision.

SEAN. How can you make a well thought out decision overnight?

AMY. Because I didn't drink myself to sleep like you did. I just did some thinking and did what I had to do. Phone please.

SEAN. I want to work this out with you.

AMY. I worked it out without you.

SEAN. Look, I know I upset you. Let's –

AMY. Stop saying that. I'm not upset. I'm not emotional

and your old tricks aren't going to work on me this time. Give me my phone.

SEAN. Let's get some brunch and talk this out.

AMY. I just said that your old tricks won't work on me.

SEAN. We'll go to the diner and go for a walk in the park.

AMY. Just give me my phone.

SEAN. If I give you the phone you'll stay?

AMY. No.

SEAN. Then you're not getting it.

AMY. Give me my phone now!

SEAN. See. You are emotional.

AMY. You're making me angry.

SEAN. That's emotional.

AMY. I'll just get a new phone.

(She starts for the door. He jumps in front of her.)

AMY. Get away from me.

SEAN. If you do this, don't call me later.

AMY. Okay.

SEAN. I'm serious, Amy. If you leave, that's it because this is downright creepy. Don't think I'm going to let you move your stuff right back in here.

AMY. Are you done?

SEAN. No. And as you go, remember that you're never going to find the right guy out there. Sure, you will find some guy who will marry you, but you will never be as happy as you are with me.

AMY. You are obviously not listening. Now for the last time will you please give me my phone?

(He gives her the phone.)

AMY. Thank you. Great. Let's go two for two. Now step out of my way please.

(He steps to the side. She takes another couple of steps towards the door. He jumps in front of her again.)

SEAN. Okay. You win.

AMY. I know I do. Move.

SEAN. We can just head out right now.

AMY. Where do you think we're going?

SEAN. We'll go to Vegas. Just like we said last night. I'm serious this time.

AMY. I'm sure you are.

SEAN. So let's do it.

AMY. That offer is off the table.

SEAN. I just put it back on the table.

AMY. I've left the negotiating table and I'd like to leave this apartment sometime this century.

SEAN. But we agreed to this last night.

AMY. No, I agreed to it. You were bluffing.

SEAN. But I'm not bluffing now.

AMY. Neither am I.

SEAN. Alright. What can I do to get you to stay?

AMY. I guess you can stay in front of that door all day.

SEAN. You know what I mean.

AMY. Nothing. Nothing. This relationship is over. It's done. I'm moving on. It happens. It happens everyday to people. There comes a moment when you realize that things have gone as far as they can with a certain person and you move on. I know you understand this. You understand it all too well. Why can't you get it this time?

SEAN. Okay. Okay. If this is what you want...

AMY. It is.

SEAN. Are you sure?

AMY. Jesus Christ. Yes.

SEAN. Okay. Don't call me saying that you want to try and make things work or maybe even take the Vegas deal.

AMY. Okay.

SEAN. You're not taking me serious are you?

AMY. I think you're dead serious.

SEAN. Okay. Go.

AMY. I will if you get away from the door.

(He steps away.)

AMY. Can you move a little further back?

(He takes another step back.)

SEAN. Take care.

AMY. I will.

(She opens the door.)

SEAN. Wait.

(She stops in the doorway.)

SEAN. Maybe you should look around one more time and make sure you didn't forget anything.

AMY. I think I'm fine. You can mail me anything that you find. I'll be staying at my parents for a little bit.

SEAN. Okay.

(The door is about to shut.

SEAN grabs it. He opens it.

Her hand was still on the door knob and she's yanked back slightly.

SEAN gets on his knees as he grabs her hand.)

SEAN. Will you marry me?

AMY. Oh, now you get on your knees?

SEAN. Will you marry me?

AMY. That ship has sailed.

SEAN. Will you marry me?

AMY. NO!

SEAN. Why not?

AMY. You don't believe in it. And I no longer believe in it. You've known it for years and I just realized it.

SEAN. We'll do it exactly as you want it. In a church or a temple or with a rabbi and a priest and in a big palatial place with tons of people and bridesmaids and ring bearers and every tradition known to man.

AMY. And it would mean nothing to me and nothing to you.

SEAN. It doesn't mean anything that I want to spend the rest of my life with you?

AMY. It's nice that you do. But as we discussed last night, you can't promise that. And neither can I. And I'm really leaving this –

SEAN. Goddmanit! What is the matter with you? You win. You've scared the shit out of me. Are you happy now?

(He gets up off his knees and retreats to the couch. She re-enters the apartment and follows him.)

AMY. Do I look happy?

SEAN. No. You don't. But you also don't look too torn up about it and I would love to see some kind of hint of emotion in you. You look like a robot like my fucking father. You're walking out on me after almost three years over one stupid drunken argument and you don't seem to care at all.

AMY. Of course I care. And it isn't one argument, Sean. This gap, this difference between us has always been there and I just ignored it and thought it would go away. More dumb cliched thinking by me. I thought that "love conquers all." But you're right. They lie to us. They lie to us through their teeth and set us up with such false hope and expectations.

SEAN. I'd appreciate it if you would stop quoting me.

AMY. Don't flatter yourself. I do have my own thoughts. And I'll share one with you right now. I asked myself an important question last night regarding this whole marriage thing, and I decided to give myself an honest answer and I wasn't happy with it. I wondered that if by some chance there was a law that stated that once you got married, you could never get out it, that you actually had to stay with this person no matter what, no matter if he beat you or cheated on you or whatever, that it really was till death do us part, would I still get married. And the truth is, I wouldn't.

SEAN. No one would, except religious nuts and rednecks.

AMY. You're right. So what does marriage really mean?

SEAN. Nothing.

AMY. I agree.

SEAN. Then if you agree, why are you leaving?

AMY. It's more than that. It's...you're such a goddamn cynic and it hurts sometimes. And the fact that you actually convinced me that I've been an idiot for believing in all this stuff kind of bothers me a bit.

SEAN. I don't think you're an idiot and I never did. I love your optimism and your big dreams and all that I really want is to have that back right now. I never intended to drive it out of you. How do you think that makes me feel?

AMY. About as lousy as I feel. So I think we need some time apart.

SEAN. No.

AMY. They say set something free, and if it comes back to you –

SEAN. Don't recycle a cliche now.

AMY. See. You just said you wanted that part of me back.

SEAN. I do. I'm sorry.

AMY. We need some time to think and...I don't know.

SEAN. I don't think this is a good idea.

AMY. I actually believe this is all going to work out for the best.

SEAN. But we can work it out together. It seems to me that we've had a breakthrough here. We're in agreement about something pretty important and we should stay together and grow from this.

AMY. You don't get it. We don't see this the same.

SEAN. We both don't believe in marriage.

AMY. But for me it's...I'll show you.

(She walks towards the bedroom.)

SEAN. Where are you going?

AMY. I'm getting something from the bedroom. I'll be right back.

(She disappears into the bedroom.

SEAN *springs to his feet.*

He runs over and shuts the apartment door. He runs back to the couch and starts dragging it towards the door.

It makes a lot of NOISE as it drags on the floor.)

AMY (O.S.) What is that noise?

SEAN. Nothing.

*(***SEAN*** *puts the couch in front of the door to block it.*

AMY *emerges from the bedroom, magazine in hand. She's searching through the pages.)*

AMY. I'll give you a couple of examples. I have your – why did you do that? *(She notices the couch in front of the door.)*

SEAN. I don't want you running out on me. We're going to finish this.

AMY. That's sick, Sean. You have a lot of problems.

SEAN. Great. What is that in your hand?

AMY. It's your "Marriage Hearse" column.

SEAN. I asked you not to quote me anymore.

AMY. Right here you say –

SEAN. I don't want to hear it.

AMY. You say, "There's a conspiracy here. The government dangles tax breaks and health benefits in order to entice people to get married. And why? Because they know marriage is otherwise a dead issue. They are keeping it alive. No wonder they don't want to give us universal health care. If they did, then they would lose the only real reason people have anymore to get married. You see, this keeps the religious nuts happy. And it all makes sense when you think about it, doesn't it? Marriage and religion are infinitely similar and they go hand in hand. Religion is a feeble man-made attempt to try and understand something man was never meant to understand: God. Marriage is a feeble man-made attempt to try and understand something man was never meant to understand: Love."

SEAN. So? That sounds like an optimistic plea for common sense to me.

AMY. I'm not done, or should I say you're not done. You get cynical several paragraphs later. You say, "marriage is like a life support machine. Life support machines are man-made mechanisms that prolong a life-like state for a person who is for all intents and purposes dead. It just keeps them alive, suffering. Marriage licenses are no different. They are man-made mechanisms that keep a relationship that is dead, alive, causing the two people to suffer."

SEAN. Honey, I'm a writer and sometimes I need to be dramatic –

AMY. And of course, who can forget your conclusion, "as long as divorce, pre-nuptial agreements and adultery exist, and they do in spades, marriage means nothing and we all know it, so why can't we just all move on from this childish nonsense?" Very nice.

SEAN. All I'm saying is that no one else really believes in it either. Why am I the bad guy? Because I'm the one who is willing to say that the emperor has no clothes?

AMY. I didn't say you were the bad guy. And there is actually one question I've always had for you about this column. Why did you open it with this lame quote, "in the words of William Blake, "But most thro' midnight streets I hear How the youthful Harlots curse. Blasts the new-born Infant's tear. And blights with plagues the marriage hearse." Why did you quote that poem?

SEAN. It doesn't matter.

AMY. I looked it up. You know that it's about hookers and venereal disease. It doesn't even make sense in your argument.

SEAN. To me it does. Or it did. The idea that marriage is stifling and deadly...forget it. I'm not going into it.

AMY. I don't understand why people call you a humorist. You're really not that funny.

SEAN. Are you done insulting me?

AMY. Sorry. I don't mean to. I just don't know if I can be with a man who thinks this way.

SEAN. You've just made it clear you agree with me.

AMY. No. I don't buy into the institution anymore, but to call it a life support machine and stifling and deadly is just too much for me. And to suggest there is some kind of government and religious conspiracy is also a bit much. You're paranoid.

SEAN. I don't really believe there's a conspiracy. Like I just said, I'm a writer and I have to be dramatic and I have lots of thoughts and some are not very nice. Let me ask you something, you read that before you ever dated me. Why did you bother with me?

AMY. I thought I saw something more in you. I thought I could be with that. I guess I was wrong.

SEAN. Whatever you saw, it's still there. I haven't changed.

AMY. Maybe I'm the one who changed, and you're not right for me anymore. Or I'm just no longer willing to fight to find whatever it is I saw in you.

SEAN. And you really realized all of this overnight?

AMY. No. Again, over the course of our relationship. We've grown apart. And I just don't think I can go back now. It's just too awkward. It's like turning the lights on in a dark room and seeing all the roaches and rats, you can never turn the lights back off and feel the same again, can you?

SEAN. If that's what you see us as, roaches and rats, I guess I can't argue with that.

(He goes over to the couch and drags it away from the door. He walks back to the door and opens it.)

SEAN. Sorry about that. That was childish. I just...forget it. I already said it. I guess you should go. Your mom should be here any minute.

AMY. No. Probably not for a bit.

SEAN. You said she'd be here in ten minutes about fifteen minutes ago.

AMY. I lied. She'll probably be here ten minutes from now actually.

SEAN. What was the point of that?

AMY. I don't know. Why did you say you didn't believe in marriage and then propose to me twice in the past fifteen minutes?

SEAN. Like you said, I have a lot of problems. Maybe I should start working on them.

AMY. I agree. And I'm going to work on myself.

SEAN. Well you can go now. I'm not going to stop you.

AMY. Thank you.

SEAN. You're welcome.

(SEAN heads for the bedroom as she heads for the door.

He disappears into the bedroom.

She stops at the door.

She takes moment to think and turns around.)

AMY. Before I go, I just wanted to apologize for saying you weren't funny. You are. It's one of the reasons I wanted to date you.

(He emerges from the bedroom.)

SEAN. Thank you.

AMY. In fact, last night I read your column on religious rituals and it made me laugh.

SEAN. What part?

AMY. All of it. But the part I really liked was when you were saying you wanted your foreskin back and that they had no right to take it at that age. It really made me laugh because the first time I was with a gentile, I didn't know they circumcised you guys too.

SEAN. Oh yeah. They do it to all of us because this country was settled by Puritans and they claim it's for health

reasons and it's really because they think we'll masturbate more if we have the foreskin. I have to be honest.
I don't know anyone who doesn't masturbate and –

AMY. I know, I know. I read the column. It was funny. Do
you still feel the same way?

SEAN. Of course.

AMY. So if the mother of your child was a Jew, you wouldn't
bend on it?

SEAN. I think you know I wouldn't.

AMY. What about baptism and all the Christian rituals? If
you had a kid would you do that to him or her?

SEAN. If I were to ever have kids, I would teach them about
religion so they can be educated, but I would never
put them through any bullshit superstitious rituals. I
would never do that to someone I love.

AMY. I guess I should go. My mom will really be here in a
few minutes.

SEAN. Tell her I said hi.

AMY. I will.

SEAN. Okay. I'll see you soon hopefully.

AMY. Hopefully.

SEAN. Alright. Goodbye.

AMY. Bye.

(They look at each other for a beat.)

SEAN. Are you going to go?

AMY. Yes.

SEAN. Okay. So...go..

AMY. No.

(She looks like she's on the verge of tears.)

AMY. I don't want to go.

(She breaks down.

SEAN *runs to her, but stops a few feet from her.)*

SEAN. I don't want you to go.

AMY. I know. But I have to.

SEAN. No you don't.

AMY. I do. After all this I can't just sit at dinner with you and lay in bed with you and do all the things we used to do.

SEAN. Yes you can.

AMY. No I can't. Because you could leave me and I could leave you.

SEAN. You had your chance why didn't you leave?

AMY. Because I love you.

SEAN. I love you too. And that's why I haven't left.

(He gets closer to her and gets face to face with her.)

This is the way it's supposed to be. You don't want to leave me but you can. You could have left at any point in the past few years and I could have to. But I didn't and you didn't. And there's no contract keeping either of us here. Don't you get that yet?

AMY. I do. But I'm scared.

SEAN. I'm scared too. But what we have is special. It's... it's....hold on, come here for a minute.

(He takes her hand and leads her to the middle of the apartment.)

SEAN. Wait right here. Don't leave. Are you going to leave?

AMY. No. I'll wait for you.

(He heads for the bedroom.

We hear him shuffling around.)

SEAN (O.S.) Just a few more seconds. Alright. I'm coming out. Close your eyes.

(He sticks his head out the door.)

Are your eyes closed?

AMY. Yes.

(She closes her eyes.

He comes out of the bedroom. He grabs a pillow cushion off the couch and places it on the floor in front of her. He kneels on it.

He pulls an engagement ring out of from behind his back.)

SEAN. Okay. Open your eyes.

(She sees the ring. Her eyes blast wide open.)

AMY. What is this?

SEAN. This is –

AMY. I said I wasn't going to marry you –

SEAN. Let me –

AMY. You're starting this whole thing over –

SEAN. Let me finish please, you lunatic.

AMY. Alright. I'm sorry.

SEAN. When my grandmother died, she gave this to me, hoping I would one day give it to someone special. My grandfather gave it to her when he proposed to her.

AMY. But you're not asking me to marry you?

SEAN. No. She just said she wanted me to give it to someone special.

AMY. I'm sure she meant when you proposed.

SEAN. Well, too bad. Times change. I'm giving this to a woman that I'm crazy about, because this ring means something to me. And I want it to mean something to you.

(He slides it on to her finger.)

AMY. Where did you hide this?

SEAN. Do you promise to stay with me and be with me and love me every single day we choose to be together?

AMY. Yes.

SEAN. Do you promise to be with only me while we choose to be together?

AMY. Yes.

SEAN. If you ever fall out of love with me, do you promise to let me go?

AMY. Yes.

(She kneels down in front of him.)

AMY. Do you promise to stay with me and be with me and love me every single day we choose to be together?

SEAN. Yes.

AMY. Do you promise to be with only me while we choose to be together?

SEAN. Yes.

AMY. If you ever fall out of love with me, do you promise to let me go?

SEAN. Yes.

(They start kissing.

They stop.

He kisses her again. He laughs a little.)

AMY. What are you laughing at?

SEAN. You. You're crazy. You know that, right?

AMY. I'd have to be to be with you.

SEAN. But you're a little less crazy than everyone else I know.

AMY. I wish I could say the same for you.

(He laughs and kisses her.

It gets really passionate now.

She starts getting into it.

They're in bliss.

Her cell phone RINGS with that annoying ring. That snaps them out of it.

She looks down at her phone.)

AMY. My mom is here. What is she going to say about all this?

SEAN. She'll ask why you can't just find a nice Jewish boy already.

*(**AMY** answers the phone.)*

AMY. Ma?...upstairs...what are we doing? Hang on.

(Back to **SEAN***)*

What do I tell her? What are we doing?

SEAN. Tell her you'll call her right back.

AMY. Mom, I'll call you right back.

(She hangs up the phone.

SEAN's *face lights up as if an amazing thought has just come over him.)*

SEAN. Here's what we're going to do. We're going to get in your mom's car, get her to drive to Long Island, pick up your dad and my mom and go to brunch.

AMY. Okay...

SEAN. And they're going to see that ring on your finger and we're going to announce that three months from now, on our actual three year anniversary, we're going to have a party to celebrate this, *(he points to the ring)* and at that party, in front of all of our friends and family, we're going to make the same promises to each other that we just made. And it won't make any sense to any of them. And then you and me can hop into a limo and head right to the airport and go to the Bahamas or something.

AMY. A non-honeymoon?

SEAN. Exactly.

AMY. And we're hiring a photographer and you're getting a tux.

SEAN. And the whole thing won't mean a damn thing to anybody but you and me; the only people who matter in this relationship.

AMY. You know your mom's head will explode.

SEAN. So will yours when she finds out that her grandson is not getting circumcised.

AMY. Oh, so you do want to have kids?

SEAN. We'll cross that bridge when we get to it.

AMY. Oh we'll get to it.

(They start kissing again.

They get very passionate again.

They're in bliss again.

Her cell phone RINGS again with that annoying ring.

That snaps them out of it.)

AMY. Oh God.

SEAN. Go ahead. Answer it.

(She clicks the phone off.)

AMY. She can wait.

(They kiss. They get very passionate again.

They're in bliss again.

No one interrupts them this time.

The lights go down.)

Also by
Matt Morillo...

Angry Young Women in Low-Rise Jeans with High-Class Issues

EVIL DEAD: THE MUSICAL
Book & Lyrics By George Reinblatt
Music By Frank Cipolla/Christopher Bond
Melissa Morris/George Reinblatt

Musical Comedy / 6m, 4f / Unit set
Based on Sam Raimi's 80s cult classic films, *Evil Dead* tells the tale of 5 college kids who travel to a cabin in the woods and accidentally unleash an evil force. And although it may sound like a horror, its not! The songs are hilariously campy and the show is bursting with more farce than a Monty Python skit. *Evil Dead: The Musical* unearths the old familiar story: boy and friends take a weekend getaway at abandoned cabin, boy expects to get lucky, boy unleashes ancient evil spirit, friends turn into Candarian Demons, boy fights until dawn to survive. As musical mayhem descends upon this sleepover in the woods, "camp" takes on a whole new meaning with uproarious numbers like "All the Men in my Life Keep Getting Killed by Candarian Demons," "Look Who's Evil Now" and "Do the Necronomicon."

Outer Critics Circle nomination for
Outstanding New Off-Broadway Musical

"The next Rocky Horror Show!"
- New York Times

"A ridiculous amount of fun."
- Variety

"Wickedly campy good time."
- Associated Press

FEMININE ENDING
Sarah Treem

Full Length / Dark Comedy / 3m, 2f / Various, Unit set
Amanda, twenty-five, wants to be a great composer. But at the moment, she's living in New York City and writing advertising jingles to pay the rent while her fiancée, Jack pursues his singing career. So when Amanda's mother, Kim, calls one evening from New Hampshire and asks for her help with something she can't discuss over the phone, Amanda is only too happy to leave New York. Once home, Kim reveals that she's leaving Amanda father and needs help packing. Amanda balks and ends up (gently) hitting the postman, who happens to be her first boyfriend. They spend the night together in an apple orchard, where Amanda tries to tell Billy how her life got sidetracked. It has something to do with being a young woman in a profession that only recognizes famous men. Billy acts like he might have the answer, but doesn't. Neither does Amanda's mother. Or, for that matter, her father. A Feminine Ending is a gentle, bittersweet comedy about a girl who knows what she wants but not quite how to get it. Her parents are getting divorced, her fiancée is almost famous, her first love reappears, and there's a lot of noise in her head but none of it is music. Until the end.

"Darkly comic. *Feminine Ending* has undeniable wit."
- New York Post

"Appealingly outlandish humor."
- The New York Times

"Courageous. The 90-minute piece swerves with nerve and naivete. Sarah Treem has a voice all her own."
- Newsday

THE SCENE
Theresa Rebeck

Little Theatre / Drama / 2m, 2f / Interior Unit Set
A young social climber leads an actor into an extra-marital affair, from which he then creates a full-on downward spiral into alcoholism and bummery. His wife runs off with his best friend, his girlfriend leaves, and he's left with… nothing.

"Ms. Rebeck's dark-hued morality tale contains enough fresh insights into the cultural landscape to freshen what is essentially a classic boy-meets-bad-girl story."
- *New York Times*

"Rebeck's wickedly scathing observations about the sort of self-obsessed New Yorkers who pursue their own interests at the cost of their morality and loyalty."
- *New York Post*

"The Scene is utterly delightful in its comedic performances, and its slowly unraveling plot is thought-provoking and gut-wrenching."
- *Show Business Weekly*

Printed in the United States
203224BV00008B/13-39/P